WARNING

This book contains sexually explicit scenes and adult language. It may be considered offensive to some readers. This book is for sale to adults ONLY.

* * * * * * * * * * * * * * * * *

Please store your files wisely where they cannot be accessed by underage readers.

ISBN-13: 978-1987863710
ISBN-10: 1987863712

Other books by Shyla Starr:

<u>Persuasive Billionaire BWWM Romance Series</u>

Stacey is trying to keep a handle on her life the best that she can. She is on the verge of losing her job and her apartment, while taking care of her sick grandmother. Her life takes an unexpected turn when she meets Charlie, who works for the construction company that is attempting to persuade her to move out of her home.

<u>Tenacious Billionaire BWWM Romance Series</u>

Adalia is too proud to accept help from the billionaire playboy, Trent Dawson. How long can she maintain her resolve? The bank is at her heels to repossess her business. To make matters worse, Adalia finds suspicious evidence of Trent's philandering ways. She must determine whether to trust Trent with the fate of her business and her heart.

<u>Elusive Billionaire Romance Series</u>

Billionaire Hendrick is trying to repair his company's image by putting in some volunteer work, building a school and hospital for the impoverished children in Africa. There, he meets a beautiful African American volunteer, Jocelyn. They hit it off right away but does she belong in his world?

<u>Lonely Billionaire Romance Series</u>

Tricia was hired to care for billionaire John's wife, who is dying. An unlikely romance emerges after his wife, Rebecca, gives John permission to pursue his happiness after she is gone.

<u>Ardent Billionaire Romance Series</u>

Deirdre doesn't know what to make of the gorgeous man that seems to be interested in her. His name is Parker Walters and he seems friendly enough. There is just something off about him. Why is he trying the hide the fact that he is the heir to his father's billion dollar software empire?

<u>Fervent Billionaire BWWM Romance Series</u>

Alexandra had never been with a white man before. She had seen William at the café before but she always kept her distance. It was unfortunate that their first chance meeting happened when she dropped her breakfast and spilled coffee all over his expensive business suit.

Get the latest update on new releases from the author at:

https://shylastarr.com/newsletter/

This book is Part Two of the "Audacious Billionaire BWWM Romance Series"

1 - Love Eluded

Chante is torn between staying close to a man beyond her league, and fleeing from him to spare herself from a hopeless position. But she finds she is propelled into a place where she needs to confront her doubts and cast her fate aside to follow the dictates of her heart. Damned if she does and miserable is she doesn't, how will Chante face the events that will lead her to a place of pure happiness or to the pits of a broken heart?

2 - Love Astray

Chante is slowly getting over her heartbreak from the enigmatic Jared Lowell. Realizing that he is not the right man for her, she is ready to fall in love again and finds happiness once more in the arms of her new lover, Dr. Leo Cadman. That is until Jared's presence at the hospital stirs up all the emotions she used to have for him. Torn between the affections of a man who adores her and a sexual attraction she cannot contradict, who will Chante gamble her heart with?

3 - Love Abided

Chante finds herself accepting a marriage proposal from a man everybody considers 'the perfect man'. She knows she is the luckiest woman on earth. But although she could fool everyone else, she could never fool herself. Her heart belongs to Jared Lowell. It always had since the day she first laid eyes on him. Caught between a farce of an engagement and a growing intimacy between her and Jared, which will win in the battle for the truth... her heart or her mind?

Audacious Billionaire BWWM Romance Series

Love Astray

Book Two

By Shyla Starr

Table of Contents

Chapter One

"**ARE WE** doing spring cleaning?" Markey Green asked his sister Chante as he eyed the clothes strewn all over her bedroom floor.

"What? No…no…no…" Chante replied, as she pulled another hanger from inside her clothes drawer.

"I just need to find the right one…" she added as she positioned the dress in front of her and stared at her reflection in the mirror.

She shook her head in disapproval. "Too revealing," she muttered under her breathe.

Markey advanced slowly into his sister's bedroom. He didn't want his wheelchair to run into the dresses that were piled haphazardly on the floor.

"Must be a hot date then," he smiled with amusement as his sister began to attack the shelves where her shoes rested.

Chante stopped momentarily. She was surprised at her brother's spontaneous perception. She smiled trying to mask the concern in her eyes. He had grown so much thinner these last few months. His ALS had progressed so much faster than she thought.

"And what do you know about having a hot date, hmmm…" she said as she tousled his hair.

"Well…enough to notice that you're excited once again. These last few months you just seemed… sad." Markey replied.

Chante felt a twinge of guilt. She honestly didn't realize her brother noticed at all.

"Was I that bad…" she asked as she sat down on the bed.

"Bad? Nah, you were just sad." Markey answered wryly.

"Yeah, I guess I was…but I'm ok now…so don't you worry about me kid." Chante replied.

She never told him about the way she felt. In fact she hasn't told anyone about it. Who would believe her anyway? It isn't everyday that a good-looking and wealthy... very wealthy... Jared Lowell asked you to be his sex toy.

Chante tried to forget everything that happened that day on the roof deck of NY General Hospital. She remembered him calling her name as she pushed the metal doors aside and ran towards the freight elevator. She punched the button on the lift and went all the way to the basement where she knew she would be safe. She was confused, her mind was in a whirl, and she wanted to stay away from prying eyes. She stopped by a wall and there amidst rows of empty cars she slumped down on the hard cement floor as despair and disillusionment brought waves of tears that shook her to the core.

"How dare he…" she muttered disconsolately, "he must think I'm scum."

Jared Lowell, heir to the fortunes of Lowell Enterprises had just offered to keep her as a mistress in exchange for a condo and for "stuff" as he called it, even having the impudence to conclude "that's what girls like…"

But Chante didn't have the heart to put all the censure on the scoundrel. She was partly to blame too, remembering what happened between them in the bathroom of the suite where his mother was a patient.

"Shit…" she whispered between her tears.

But it was too late now for regrets. It happened and she had to live with it. In hindsight, she was confused why she even allowed it to come about. Had the patient, Samantha Lowell, or Nurse Betty, and Director Whittle come back and caught them in the illicit act, she would have lost her job as Certified Nursing Assistant, that's for sure.

It was with uncertainty that she reported for work the very next day. She had vowed the night before that she would refuse adamantly, beg even, not to be assigned to Suite 247 once again. But the floor seemed unusually quiet that morning. She learned that Samantha Lowell was discharged the night before. The private helicopter that brought her in brought her out, as well.

"Oh, thank God," was Chante's initial reaction.

She didn't have to suffer the awkwardness of seeing Jared again. Admittedly, she liked Mrs. Lowell. She felt a certain degree of kinship with the older woman. It made her a little sad, thinking she didn't get a chance to say goodbye.

But as the initial relief swept through her body, she was also assailed with a deep sense of melancholy. She won't be seeing Jared Lowell anymore. That, at least, was its own blessing, Chante thought.

The weeks that followed their departure, Chante often had to struggle with her feelings. She tried to focus on her work but often found herself looking out into space. She felt miserable, disconnected, and it took all her effort to keep going about her duty. The world lay heavily on her shoulders.

Nurse Betty took her aside and asked what was bothering her. Chante couldn't look her in the eye. The woman was very perceptive.

"Is this about a man?" Nurse Betty inquired.

Chante nodded her head. The supervisor didn't have to know who. So Chante decided on a half-lie.

"Yes…but it's over now…" Chante answered.

"That's good. If it didn't last too long, then he must be the wrong guy for you. Get out of that hole you crawled into. Someone better should come along for you." The supervisor consoled her.

Chante nodded her head in agreement. Nurse Betty didn't know how close to the truth she was. Jared Lowell was definitely the wrong guy for her. It's about time she moved on and forgot all about him.

Things were slowly getting back to normal.

One day, Chante was assigned to the Emergency Room. One of the nurses on duty was down with the flu. The ER head called on Nurse Betty if she had anyone to spare for an 8-hour shift.

Nurse Betty was hesitant to send Chante. She didn't have enough experience with trauma. But the ER head assured her that it was only to help out with minor tasks- cleaning wounds, putting on bandages, administering anesthetics. The other RNs and doctors could take care of the rest.

Chante entered a frenzied ER. It was chaotic. The waiting room was filled with people- mothers and fathers, a sister or brother, or someone's cousin- all waiting for a doctor to tell them about the condition of a patient that was brought in.

The six beds were filled. One patient was having an intubation procedure done; another bed had an old man with a nurse having difficulty locating a vein for IV placement. The old man was agitated and kept pulling his arm away. Another doctor was accompanying a patient out for transport by medical helicopter.

Chante immediately got to work gathering bandages, towels, and cotton balls when the door burst open. A distraught woman had a child in her arms.

Chante rushed over. The child was convulsing and his eyes rolled towards the top of his head. There was no bed available to put him in.

Chante noticed a trolley earlier just outside the ER entrance. She ran quickly and pushed it towards the woman and her child. A doctor, who was busy sewing up a knife victim, hurriedly took note of the child's condition. The child convulsed once again.

"Nurse… nurse… ", the doctor shouted at Chante. "Get Dr. Leonard Cadman… tell him it's a possible status epilepticus. He's at the doctor's lounge sleeping. GO!"

"Doctor's lounge…doctor's lounge…it must be somewhere near," Chante mumbled under her breath as she ran out of the ER and into the hallway.

She turned a corner and saw the sign on a door and hoped this was the right one. She opened it hurriedly. The room was dark and Chante had to adjust her eyes before she saw a figure huddled on a bed farthest from the door. She approached slowly not wanting to wake up the wrong doctor.

The man was sleeping on his right side and facing the wall. Chante couldn't tell by his name plate that was hidden beneath his crossed arms, if this was THE Doctor Cadman she was asked to call immediately.

Not wanting to spare another second, Chante called out, "Dr. Cadman…"

No response. The man was in deep sleep. But she did notice that this guy was olive-skinned with a crown of cornrows that framed a chiseled face. Thick long lashes fanned out on cheeks that were crunched by the pillow that was under his head.

Chante knew she had to rouse him sooner than later, so she touched a leg that was sprawled on the bed.

"Dr. Cadman…" Chante called out louder this time.

The figure on the bed stirred, opened his eyes, and looked towards her.

Chante had the image of charcoal grey eyes the color of clouds on a stormy day.

"I'm sorry…but if you are Dr. Leonard Cadman, there is a possible status epilepticus in the ER." Chante mouthed the words.

With one swift move, Dr. Cadman was out of bed and on his feet. He searched for his stethoscope that was lying by the floor where he must have dropped it.

Chante saw this doctor was medium built, taller than she was by a few inches, and was a bundle of energy now that he was awake.

"Sex…" he said.

"What?" Chante replied, before she realized he was asking about the patient's gender.

"Boy…about six years old." Chante answered back hoping he didn't notice her initial confusion.

She followed him out the door as he scurried to the ER.

There were no regular nurses available to assist Dr. Cadman so Chante thought she would stay nearby in case he needed assistance.

"How long ago was his last seizure?" the doctor barked at the hysterical mother. She stared back at him as if he had spoken gibberish.

"How long…?" Dr. Cadman repeated.

"Less than 5 minutes ago," Chante made a wild guess, realizing the mother was absolute no help in this scenario.

"Nurse…I need 5cc of…" the doctor said just as Chante rushed to the medicine cabinet.

She knew exactly what he needed- a prefilled syringe with the medication. She was thankful for all the times her mom allowed her inside the medical tent when they were doing medical mission work.

She handed him the syringe, grasped the boy by the neck tilting his head upwards, and opened his mouth to allow the doctor access inside the opening.

"Thanks…" Dr. Cadman said seeing her clearly for the first time.

The effect of the medicine was instantaneous. After 2 minutes the boy's body visibly relaxed and his breathing though still ragged, was slowly getting back to normal.

The little boy reached out and the doctor clasped the small hand with his.

Chante saw the concern and compassion for the little boy who was scared and confused over what just happened.

"It's alright, you'll be alright…your momma is here…" the doctor cooed softly to the boy.

The hysterical mother had calmed down sufficiently to hug her son while repeatedly saying, "thank you…thank you…"

"Nurse…" Dr. Cadman addressed her.

"Err…I'm not actually a registered nurse," Chante explained, "I was sent here to assist. I'm just a CNA."

"What the…" Dr. Cadman replied with surprise.

He didn't have enough time to finish his sentence as the door to the ER banged open once again with a bloody patient on a trolley.

"White, male, approx 26 years old, stab wound on the lower abdomen…" announced the EMT.

It was total chaos for Chante. Emergency cases after another just kept on coming. She lost track of Dr. Cadman as Chante was asked to bandage a patient, administer IV on another, ran to the pharmacy, and comfort distraught relatives.

A few hours later she found herself working side by side with the doctor again. Chante noticed how efficient he was at what he did, often stopping to give a word of comfort to the patient or to a family member. He kept on addressing Chante as "Nurse" giving her instructions what to do after every procedure. Chante followed orders. She could just correct the misimpression at a later time.

Hours flew by very swiftly before a palpable calm finally settled on the otherwise frenetic atmosphere. Chante realized most of the doctors she saw were new arrivals. She thought now was a good time to go. She just needed to inform the ER head nurse she was calling it a night.

"You did very well today considering…" a familiar voice spoke out behind her.

Chante turned around and saw Dr. Cadman had changed from his scrubs to a pair of faded jeans and a white t-shirt. He held a leather jacket in another hand. If Chante didn't know better, she would have mistaken him for a rock star or a member of a band.

"Uhhm…thanks, Dr. Cadman, " Chante answered, as an overwhelming shyness overcame her.

She wondered why the simple remark made her feel good.

"Leo…the name is Leo, Miss…Green," he added after eyeing her nameplate.

"Chante, please call me Chante…" she replied. "And as I said earlier, I'm not an RN."

"I admit you did take me by surprise when you mentioned that earlier. So tell me, Ms. NOT RN Chante. How come you knew what I needed back then with the child?" Leo asked with a twinkle in his eye.

"My adoptive parents were medical missionaries. I grew up seeing convulsive children almost every day. It just came back to me. That's how come I knew," Chante explained.

Leo's grey eyes travelled up and down her face, taking in the exhausted emerald eyes and said, "I see that you are on your way out. Maybe you'd like to have coffee. To tell you the truth I don't remember when my last meal was. I've been on a sixteen-hour shift."

"I really should be on my way…" Chante hesitated.

She couldn't understand why the simple invitation somehow managed to take away some of the fatigue she felt.

"Please…" Leo begged, "I hate eating alone and I promise to drop you off."

"Well…alright then…I'll just get my stuff and meet you in the parking lot," Chante replied as a kind of thrill bloomed in the pit of her stomach.

She immediately changed into her street clothes regretting the fact she didn't bring something nicer to wear. But how could she have known that an attractive-looking doctor would be asking her out to dinner tonight?

She pulled back the rubber band that was holding her hair in a severe bun and allowed the tresses to fall softly onto her shoulder. Clutching her ID, she swiped her time card against the machine and was soon on her way out the back door.

Leo was waiting by a silver-gray Lexus Hybrid, slouched against the hood with his left foot bent back against the grill of the car.

"God…he is sexy…" Chante concluded.

One couldn't describe Dr. Leo Cadman a stud, but his physique showed he did hit the gym. The lean arms were devoid of any adornment except for a silver wrist watch. The V-necked t-shirt that replaced the scrubs from earlier displayed a compact chest that was wide against a narrow waist. The butt was solid and round, sloping down towards firm thighs and sockless feet shod in brown Brooks Walkers.

He immediately straightened once he noticed Chante approaching. He ushered her towards the passenger side of the Lexus and opened the door for her.

"Gallant…" Chante whispered in her head as Leo reached across and strapped her in, his hands brushing softly against the front of her dress.

Chante followed his movements with her eyes as he moved towards the front of the car and onto the driver side before he opened the door and slid in.

"Do you have anywhere in mind…to get a bite to eat, I mean?" He asked in a low mellow voice.

"Please…you decide," Chante suggested. "After all, you're the one who is hungry."

"Great…" Leo replied as he turned the engine and slowly maneuvered out of the parking lot.

Chante found herself mesmerized by the hands that grasped the steering wheel. She had to admit that Dr. Leo Cadman had the longest set of fingers she had ever seen in a man. He could have been a pianist. And she appreciated how efficient those fingers had been as he took care of his patients earlier at the ER.

He popped a disc into the CD player and Norah Jones singing "Come Rain or Come Shine" filled the inside of the car.

Chante relaxed back into the seat feeling the weariness slowly evaporate from her tired body. Instinctively, she knew that there was no need for small talk just now. She really didn't know how she knew, but she felt absolutely at ease in the presence of the doctor she just met a few hours ago?

"The exact opposite of how Jared Lowell made me feel," the thought came unbidden to her mind.

Chante realized she was thinking of him again. She sighed deeply unaware that she made a sound.

"Are you alright, Chante?" Leo asked with concern, "If you're exhausted, I can take you home right now…"

"No... no… no… please, it's just something I remembered suddenly. It's not important really…not anymore…" Chante replied.

"I'm glad…" Leo replied back, noticing the resolute thrust of her chin and the beautiful eyes that wanted to reassure him everything was fine.

They drove for another fifteen minutes. New York traffic wasn't so bad. Leo drove to a café that was set back against an arbor of trees in the background. It was a quieter part of town. There were a few cars parked along the side of the road.

"This is where I usually go when I want good food. Their barbecued ribs are to die for." Leo informed her.

They entered a cozy bar with wooden tables spread across the interior. The wall lamps cast a soft glow across the dimly lit room. There were a few people around having a late dinner. Soft piped- in music added to the warm atmosphere of the restaurant.

Leo chose a table further away from most of the diners. Chante was elated, but again, she didn't understand why.

A waiter approached and Leo ordered for both of them. Chante was glad he did that. It felt like he was in charge of everything… and that made her feel pampered, like he knew what pleased her.

After the waiter had gone, Leo inched forward, positioned both elbows on the table, crossed the fingers of his hand, and rested his chin against them. He looked straight at her without saying a word.

Chante found his gaze made her self-conscious as she swept away an imaginary hair to the back of her ear.

"Enchanting Chante…," he murmured under his breath but loud enough for her to hear.

"Tell me all about you," he coaxed her.

And for the first time in a very long while, Chante felt her heart beat again. She tried not to put too much meaning into his words, but somehow Chante knew this guy was different. He was kind, caring, sweet and thoughtful. So different from…

But Chante didn't want to go there just now. In fact she was determined to move on and away from that memory. And the man in front of her appeared to want to come along to wherever her journey had begun.

Chapter Two

"So…is it a hot date?" Markey insisted after his sister had been silent for a few minutes.

"Uhmm…yes…its Leo Cadman. Remember him? He brought me home one night and you were still up," Chante reminded him.

"Oooh… the rock star? He's cool," Markey replied, remembering.

"He's not a rock star silly. He's an ER doctor." Chante corrected him.

Chante hadn't told her brother that she had been seeing Leo for some time now. After the late dinner, she wasn't expecting to see him again even if both worked in the same hospital. She didn't want to raise her expectations and be disappointed again. But during that particular night, Leo proved to be a good listener.

Chante found herself telling him about her early years, the succession of foster homes before she was finally adopted by the Greens, Markey's unexpected arrival into their lives, her parents' death, and her struggles in coping with Markey's ALS.

Leo wasn't only a good listener, but he was funny too. Chante found herself laughing over his experiences before he decided to become a doctor. He confided that he found his true calling working at the ER. The hours were long, but the gratification was instant, he said. If he was instrumental in making a patient live another day, he was content.

He made no mention of a girlfriend and Chante didn't see a ring on his finger so she assumed he was single…and available. Again, she curtailed the optimism that was forming inside her chest.

He was true to his word and dropped her off at her place. Chante was pleasantly surprised when Leo asked if he could come in and see her brother for a little while.

Markey didn't say much as he reached out to shake Leo's extended hand. He was probably more taken aback to see a dark stranger inside their living room. Chante ushered him out the door shortly after.

"Thanks for tonight…" Leo said as he bent forward giving her a peck on the cheeks.

Chante's face turned red as a warm heat suffused her cheeks. She hurriedly closed the door and hoped he didn't notice.

Leo sent a text message the next day asking to meet for coffee at the hospital cafeteria. Chante thought, why not? The cafeteria was a safe place… it meant thirty minutes for a coffee break.

The problem with a hospital cafeteria is the presence of knowing eyes that tend to put more into something uncomplicated as having coffee. Chante returned to the nurse's station and was ribbed endlessly about the sexy doctor she had coffee with. She denied vehemently that there was more to it than that, but she couldn't deny the warm buzz that enveloped her the rest of the day.

She didn't hear from him for the rest of the week. Chante was torn between calling him and dropping by the ER.

"He's probably too busy…," Chante reasoned out.

"…or on extended shift…," she consoled herself.

"…or it's his day off…," she thought feeling slightly dejected.

"…or he is not interested in seeing me anymore…," Chante concluded.

So it was to her utter delight as she stood by the hospital sidewalk waiting for the bus that would bring her home, a silver-grey Lexus cruised its way to where she stood.

Leo Cadman was just as gorgeous as ever. The corn rows were gone… instead his head was a crown of frizzy hair that tumbled gently down the nape of his neck.

He had no explanation for his long absence and Chante didn't ask. She was just glad to see him again. They had dinner at the same café, and she received the same gentle peck on the cheek when he said goodnight.

They saw each other again for the next couple of days, caught a movie, went bowling, and had coffee at the cafeteria, almost every afternoon.

Chante didn't know what their relationship status was. Leo always seemed eager to see her and was warm and engrossed with her company. He never tried to put his arms around her or hold her hand, which confused Chante incessantly. Did he like her or not. Was he just being a total gentleman? Should she make the first move to bring their relationship to the next level, she asked herself.

That was the reason she was in a state of confusion over the hot date tonight. She didn't want to seem too forward and be rejected. But she wanted to send the message across that she was open if he was interested.

Leo said he would take her dancing.

Chante settled for a little black mini dress that had a low neckline. She donned a pair of sheer stockings and high heeled shoes. She hoped he would find it sexy and not think she was going to a funeral.

Markey suggested she wore a gold bangle bracelet as her only accessory. She gathered her hair to the side in a messy chignon style and allowed the rest to fall softly across her shoulders.

"WOOT! WOOT!" Markey tweeted.

Chante was glad he approved as she stepped out of her bedroom.

The doorbell rang and Chante tried to stifle the nervous energy she felt.

Leo's face was a picture of dumbfounded surprise and appreciation. Frankly he had never seen her in anything but the ubiquitous hospital scrubs or jeans and a tee-shirt.

"You… you… you look ravishing Chante." Leo whispered.

Chante noticed the pupils of his eyes dilate. As they stepped out into the sidewalk to get to his car, Chante was alarmingly aware of his hand on her elbow that slowly slid downwards to hold her hand.

He took her to a posh ballroom dancing club in Long Island. The place was huge with round tables covered in white brocade cloth and an Ikea center piece lantern. The center of the room was hardwood floor that shone and reflected the lights of the lanterns on each table. A twenty piece orchestra was set back against one wall fronting the dance floor.

Chante felt like Cinderella. Leo chose a table for two and ordered a bottle of champagne. Holding the flute in her hand, Chante took a sip and immediately felt the bubbly go straight to her knees, turning them to jelly.

"I… I really don't dance, you know…" Chante confessed.

Leo gave her an enigmatic smile but said nothing. He seemed perfectly content watching the other couples dance The Swing, Cha-cha, or Tango their way around the ballroom.

Chante felt a slight disappointment. She would have loved at least to try it. Maybe they were here just to watch.

After a short break, the orchestra signaled the start of another piece. As the trumpet signaled the opening strains of "Moonlight Serenade," Leo pushed back his chair and reached out his hand asking for a dance.

"I don't know how to dance…" Chante repeated.

"Follow my lead…" Leo replied.

Chante walked with him to the dance floor. He held her right hand with his left and wrapped his other arm across her waist drawing her near. Chante stumbled in her haste to follow his lead. His proximity was giving her anxiety.

"Close your eyes and listen to the music… let me do the rest…" He whispered in her ear.

Chante did as she was told and relaxed. The music was poignant and very arousing. He was a smooth dancer. The arm across her back felt hot against the fabric of her dress. His thigh prodded hers towards the direction where his next step would lead them. Chante caught his rhythm and realized she could dance.

His groin would touch hers inadvertently and Chante had to control the impulse to gasp as she felt the firmness of what was inside those pants. She felt what she thought was the touch of his lips on her neck just above her shoulder. But she wasn't sure if it was a kiss. She realized she was thinking too much and decided to just lose herself in the music.

Leo brought her hand that was in his towards the back of his neck. He then lowered his own arm to join the other arm that was around her waist. Chante felt him draw her even nearer to him as she lifted her face to his. The look in his eyes told her what she needed to know. He felt something and it was exactly what she was feeling too.

The rest of the dance was a blur in Chante's mind. Both were consumed by a primal urge that needed to be satisfied. When the music ended, Leo paid the bill and they were soon inside his car. Without a word spoken between them, he started the engine and drove like his ass was on fire.

They ended up in his apartment, and as soon as the door closed behind them, he pressed her against the wall, his eyes never leaving hers, his breath panting against his half-opened mouth. With the wall on her back and his entire body pressed tightly against hers, Chante felt his cock through the thin fabric of her dress. She wiggled her hips slightly allowing her crotch to feel him.

Leo's lips traveled down her neck and towards her ear. She could feel his warm breath as he gently bit her on the earlobe. His hands groped for her breast as he slowly stroked her hardened nipples.

Chante's hands caressed the back of his neck as she tried to pull him closer. Every inch of her skin yearned to be caressed by his lips. She could feel the strong beating of his heart as her hands feverishly tried to open the buttons of his shirt. She fondled the front of his pants and felt the hardness of his penis.

Leo pulled her towards the bedroom and undressed her slowly before taking off his clothes. Chante could hardly breathe as she stared at his naked body. The mat of dark pubes formed a triangular pattern against his groin. He picked her up in his arms and carried her to bed. He proceeded to kiss her lips before he followed a path down to her breasts, the side of her waist, down to her navel, her thighs, knees, and then her feet.

He planted himself between her legs and opened her thighs slowly. Chante was on fire as she felt his fingers slide between her labia and caressed her clit.

"You are so beautiful," he whispered huskily.

Chante felt the exact moment his tongue went down on her. Ice and fire shot through her entire being as he flicked his tongue on her protruding clit over and over again.

Her moans filled the room as Chante clawed the sides of the bed. She angled her hips upward to allow him more access to her cunt as she resisted the urge to cum.

Chante wanted Leo inside her mouth so she could taste him and savor the feel of his cock between her lips. She twisted around to set her free and pushed him to the bed.

Chante straddled Leo and allowed her fingers to play with one of his nipples while running her tongue against the other. Then she lowered herself slowly until his penis was within inches from her mouth. She grasped him with both hands as her tongue played with the tip of his bulging member.

Chante heard his rattled breathing as she slowly sucked his penis inch by inch, until he was completely inside her mouth. She bobbed up and down his entire shaft, sucking and caressing him.

Leo reached out and pulled her up by the waist and positioned her legs between his face. Her cunt was a few inches from his mouth. Chante felt him slide open the lips of her vagina and caressed her with his tongue. Both proceeded to devour each other relentlessly.

Chante knew from Leo's grunts that he was about to come. With arms and legs entwined, Leo set her down and positioned himself on top of her. Without losing a beat, he thrust his penis into her wet pussy and rammed into her repeatedly until they both shuddered in an orgasmic frenzy.

Leo lay spent and breathing heavily, nestled in Chante's arms. She reached out and caressed the sinewy muscles in his back. She knew she had feelings for this man, but didn't know how deep it went. She had been thinking about this time, when it would happen, where, and what she had to do to get there.

Instinctively, she realized that Leo was the kind of guy who would love honestly and give the relationship all that he had. He did not seem the kind of guy who went for casual sex. Chante wondered what she truly felt about him. His detachment these past few weeks challenged her; it confused her about him. Maybe that was the reason she made herself attractive tonight. See where it would lead to.

But was she getting ahead of herself? He hasn't said anything yet.

Until…

"I love you, Chante…I think I have loved you since the day I first met you." Leo said.

Chante was stunned. Really? Was that possible?

And then she remembered Jared and how easily she fell in love with him, how much she went through to get over her feelings for him.

"Would you like us to see each other exclusively?" Leo added after she remained silent.

"You mean the boyfriend-girlfriend thing?' Chante asked with a slight smile on her lips.

"I don't do the boyfriend-girlfriend thing…" Jared's words echoed in her mind.

"Yeah…would you like that…? I mean…" Leo asked, unsure if she was laughing at him.

Chante knew that she must cross the line somewhere. She vowed to get over Jared Lowell and Leo was everything Jared Lowell was not.

"Yes…I think I'd like that…very much." Chante answered.

Leo shifted his body and cradled her in his arms.

"I'm glad…I won't ever do anything to hurt you, Chante. That's a promise." Leo said.

Chante's mind rejoiced over those words, but she wondered why her heart was not exactly jumping for joy.

Time…that was all she needed, she thought.

Sometimes it takes the heart longer to accept. But she knew she had a good thing going with Dr. Leo Cadman and she would be so foolish if she allowed her heart to rule her head and listen to that little voice telling her otherwise.

Chapter Three

"Damn…" Chante muttered under her breath as she erased an error on the application form on her desk.

She never realized how tedious it could be to answer everything in triplicate. The Board of Trustees of NY General Hospital needed every bit of information about her background… her parents, brother Markey, her entire life history, before she could be considered a candidate for scholarship.

Today was the last day of loan form submissions required by the Hospital Fund Trustee Board and she was rushing to catch the 5:00 pm deadline.

She considered herself lucky the hospital offered such scholarship grants for Certified Nursing Assistants wanting to become Registered Nurses.

She had spent the last few days searching for a school that had a bridge program. She found a community college that had a remaining slot, and she grabbed the opportunity. Then it was another stressful three days gathering the requirements for admission at the school.

Nurse Betty was happy over her decision and furnished her with a document on her Current

Employment as a Certified Nursing Assistant. She had a good working history with the hospital, Nurse Betty said.

She couldn't find her CNA Training Certificate until Markey suggested that she look in their mom's papers. It was there among old photos of her as a child. She went back to her old school and asked for a photocopy of her GPA and realized she did really well in high school.

Now all she needed was to pay the admission fee and she would be a nursing student once more. She sincerely hoped the hospital would release the funds for the scholarship immediately.

Chante inspected the hospital forms and hoped she didn't miss anything important. Nurse Betty said Director Whittle was a stickler for protocol and would probably call her within days after she submitted the loan forms.

She was glad it was over with. She had missed out on meeting up with Leo these last couple of days. She knew he understood how badly she wanted this. He said he was supporting her all the way.

"It's all in the hands of the trustees now…" Chante said to herself as she plucked out her cell to call him.

"Hey babe…" Leo's cheerful voice greeted her.

Chante realized how lucky a girl she was to have him as a boyfriend. He was caring, thoughtful, and so sweet. The other nurses were all green with envy.

Apparently, a lot of them had a secret crush on the good-looking doctor from the ER.

They constantly wheedled her about their dates, asking her to spare no details. Chante just laughed over their endless curiosity. He was hers… eat your hearts out… that's all they needed to know, she said.

"We can meet up after your shift," Chante told him over the phone, "I'm done and free and yours for the night."

"Great…" Leo answered, "See you at the lobby, uhhm around 7:00?"

"Ok, see you then…" Chante replied as she felt her phone buzz. She had a text message.

The message was short. It informed her to be at the 7th floor in ten minutes for the Trustees Board interview.

"That was quick," Chante thought.

She made her way up the banks of elevators, entered a lift and pushed the button for the 7th floor. She hoped that Director Whittle wouldn't take too long with the interview. This was just supposed to be standard procedure before a loan was released.

The seventh floor hallway had plush carpeting and was lined with doors announcing the names of the members of the board. Chante headed towards the end where she knew Director Whittle had his office.

A secretary greeted her with a smile as she pushed the door open.

"Chante Green to see Director Whittle," Chante announced.

"Oh…Director Whittle is on leave," the secretary informed her.

"But… but… I just got a text message asking me to come up here. I assumed it was for the forms I submitted earlier…about the scholarship grant…" Chante replied with some confusion.

"That's right," the secretary informed her, "please enter through that door."

Chante walked gingerly towards the closed door. If Director Whittle was not available then she was meeting someone else. Possibly another member of the board, she thought.

Chante turned the knob, opened the inner door and entered. The occupant was on a swivel chair with his back facing her. She glimpsed a stack of forms that the figure was holding in his hands.

Chante cleared her throat and said, "Err…my name is Chante Green and I was asked to come?"

The figure slowly pivoted around to face her and Chante let out a surprised gasp.

Jared Lowell was seated in the chair.

"Jared… err…I mean… Mr. Lowell…Uhmm… there must be a mista…" Chante managed to stammer.

And then she remembered.

Shit!!!

Jared Lowell was the biggest contributor for the trust fund. He probably owned the whole goddamn thing.

"Hello Chante," Jared greeted her coolly.

Chante was taken aback by the greediness of her eyes as she drunk in his appearance. He was in a three piece pin-striped suit that only managed to enhance the cobalt blue eyes. The longish hair definitely needed a haircut as it framed the patrician face.

"Well…don't just stand there. Take a seat." Jared instructed her.

Yup… still domineering, Chante thought as she urged her feet to move.

She felt an overwhelming desire to explain why she fled from him that day on the roof deck until she realized that she was not here for that. She was here because she needed money from him… from the board… so she can study to become a nurse.

She also realized the irony of her situation. He offered to keep her in a condo, buy her "stuff" which she refused. And now this?

Jared was studying the forms he held in her hand. His face was inscrutable.

"Jared, I understand if you…if the board denies my request…" Chante began.

"I'm granting it to you…" Jared said simply.

"What…?" Chante asked in bewilderment.

"The loan that you need… I'm granting it to you. There's no need to ask the board. I'll take care of it," Jared explained.

"Thank you…" Chante whispered almost on the verge of tears.

An uncomfortable silence followed. A silence that neither one knew how to fill.

"Why didn't you tell me your brother had ALS?" Jared inquired after some time.

"I… I… it just never came up, I guess," Chante replied.

Was that the reason he was being so nice to her? Because he pitied her?

Chante wanted to leave the office. Her sanity couldn't stand another second being near his presence.

"Thank you, again…I have to go…," Chante stammered as she rose from her chair.

"I'll walk you down. I'm on my way out too…" Jared replied rising from his chair.

Chante walked stiffly beside him towards the elevator. Really? This timing sucks, she thought.

The elevator doors swished shut and Chante felt the need to breathe. She didn't realize she was holding it in.

The gears of the lift seemed to grind ever sooo slowly as Chante counted the floor buttons flashing on the panel.

Sixth floor… fifth floor…fourth floor…

Chante was increasingly aware of Jared's presence in the confined space.

Third floor…Second floor…

"Would you like to have dinner with me?" Jared suddenly asked as the door opened to the lobby.

"What…?" Chante asked in sudden surprise.

"Oh... there's my girl," Leo's voice suddenly greeted them.

He approached them as Chante stayed rooted to the spot. He placed an arm across her shoulder proprietarily and drew her close.

Jared stood still, taken by surprise.

"Err…Leo…this is Jared Lowell. He just granted me the loan…Jared, this is Dr. Leo Cadman," Chante made the awkward introduction.

The two shook hands, Leo effusively, Jared stiffly.

"On behalf of my beautiful girlfriend, I'd like to say thanks. She is most deserving. Aren't you babe?" Leo declared giving Chante a tender look.

"I'm sure she is…" Jared replied coldly.

Chante watched as Jared turned to leave. She wanted to stop him… to explain why Leo's arm was across her shoulder… to ask if she heard right about him asking her out to dinner…or if she heard wrong.

But his receding figure left her with no options except to follow Leo out into his car. He was her boyfriend. He was so happy for her. And she should be too. But why did she feel so shitty instead?

Chapter Four

"What's wrong with you today, Chante?" Nurse Betty looked at her with irritation.

This was the second time she got the meds mixed up for a different patient. Her mind was spinning and she needed to focus, keep her composure, before Nurse Betty threw her out into the street.

But how could she?

Jared Lowell was in the same building, more appropriately, sitting in an office on the 7th floor, running the operation for the trust fund in the absence of Director Whittle.

Chante decided now was a good time to take a break. She wanted to gather her composure before returning to the floor. She needed her head straight before she accidentally murdered a patient.

She tried calling Leo's cell but the conversation was short. He was dealing with an emergency situation and couldn't join her for coffee.

She replayed in her mind the earlier exchange with Nurse Betty.

"Isn't that grand of him…donating his time to this hospital when he has so much to do?" Nurse Betty said in a voice that sounded like a swoon.

"You're such a lucky girl… you didn't need to face the whole board… and to get your loan in a matter of minutes? That's never happened before," Nurse Betty added.

Chante knew she shouldn't let this affect her. After all, there were five floors between them. There was no need to bump into each other by accident. She just needed to overcome the nervous tension in the pit of her stomach that was driving her insane.

Determined to concentrate more on her job, Chante returned to the Nurses' station.

"Oh…there you are," greeted Nurse Betty, "I received a call from HR. Seems like they need someone to help Mr. Lowell with all the records. I thought you might like the idea… this being a way of saying thanks for the fast release of your loan? So… I volunteered your services."

"WHAT???" Chante replied, horror written all over her face.

"What's wrong?" Nurse Betty asked, seeing the look on her face.

Chante realized she was in a no-win situation. She couldn't say no. That would make her look ungrateful. Besides, what reason could she possibly come up with for denying the request? She placed all her reserves foolishly on the five floors that were between them. But she was about to be thrown into the lion's den.

"Of course… of course… I'll do it…" Chante replied and hoped the supervisor wouldn't ask for an explanation over her initial reaction.

"Good…" Nurse Betty replied before turning back to her charts.

It was with trepidation that Chante entered the elevator on her way to the 7th floor. She glanced at her reflection on the mirrors lining the elevator wall. She wished she had the time to fix her hair or have a tube of lipstick to apply on her nude lips.

She pinched her cheeks hoping it would give her the rosy glow she wanted and realized there was no need. Her face was flushed. The thought of being near him again was unsettling. She shook her head to drive away all apprehension.

"This is work," she muttered to herself, "that's all it is…"

Jared was on the phone when she entered the office. The room was in disarray with folders and documents strewn all over. He stopped momentarily when he saw her and waved her in.

Chante didn't know whether to stand or sit. She looked at the mess on his desk and thought she should start organizing. But again, he may have done that purposely and she didn't want to create more chaos than what was already there.

"Mother says hi. She's delighted to know you're here to help…" Jared said, putting down the phone.

"Oh… oh… that's great. I hope she's feeling better," Chante replied.

Jared appeared to be all business and Chante was thankful. He told her how he needed organizing to be done, by alphabetical order, he said.

Chante went through the stacks of folders and started to file them. She wished she could do it outside by the secretary's table but it would seem silly if she brought them all out and bring them inside one by one, after she was done.

Truthfully, she wanted to be away from those eyes that followed her every move as she bent down, retrieved papers, and added them to the pile she had started.

She was about to pick up another set of papers that was on his table when he reached out his hand to stop her.

"Leave that…" he said.

Chante was stunned by the effect of his hand touching hers. She felt that familiar tingle that made the hair on her skin stand on end, like she touched an open socket.

She drew her hand away in an instant.

Jared scoffed and said, "Not so impervious after all…"

Chante decided the best defense was silence. She had nothing to say. He was right. She was just as affected now as she was when they first met.

"Tell me about that guy in the lobby. I assume he is your boyfriend? And a doctor too. Not bad Chante Green, not bad at all." Jared said.

Chante felt the hackles rise at the back of her neck. Was he mocking her? Did he mean she was not worth a doctor's attention?

She turned her back and started walking towards another pile of papers.

She faked a drool and said, "Yes, Leo is my boyfriend. He is the sweetest man I've been with and the best lover I've ever had. I'll marry him if he asks."

There…that should put him in his place, she thought. She turned around to get more documents and ran smack into him.

Jared's sardonic smile was plastered all over his face as he placed his arms around her waist and pulled her close. Chante was taken by surprise at the sudden proximity and gasped.

"Are you sure about that, Chante" Jared asked as he lowered his face down to hers.

"Jared… please…," Chante whispered as his face kept coming closer and closer.

She remembered the warmth of his lips on hers. She remembered what his tongue could do to her. It could make her forget her name.

"I could take you here on the table and you wouldn't say no…" Jared taunted her.

"Jared… please…" Chante begged.

She was unsure if she was begging him to stop or to do as he pleased. Everything was so confusing.

"What do you want me to do… kiss you perhaps?" Jared asked, his lips almost upon hers.

Chante wanted to say no, she wanted to resist him. But her body was completely disconnected from her mind. This was so wrong, her mind was telling her. But her body had taken over completely as her lips said… "Yes."

Jared lips felt like the heat of a torrid dessert. His hands moved to each side of her face and clasped her, his lips feverishly parting her mouth. Then his tongue was inside her, probing, seeking, and demanding to be familiar with him once again.

Chante felt all her senses respond to his authority. She was helpless to deny him what she knew she wanted to give without restraint, without question for any repercussions. She knew that this was where she wanted to be.

"Oh Chante, what are you doing to me…?" Jared sighed against her lips.

Chante was breathing heavily as she pushed away from him. This time she had no intentions of fleeing from him. She wanted to confront this situation head on. This was unacceptable. Leo was in her life now. She couldn't stand the thought of hurting him. He didn't deserve it. Leo Cadman was everything she ever wanted in a man.

Or was he?

Jared saw the play of emotions as it crossed her face. He knew exactly what she was thinking.

He wanted her badly. He wanted to fuck the hell out of her. He tried to forget her during all these months but found it impossible. Every girl he dated, he found wanting. The skin was the wrong color, the eyes were not green enough, and the hair was too short or too long. He morphed these women in his mind to look like Chante. But he was never satisfied.

When the chance presented itself, he grabbed at the excuse of working with the board for the trust fund here at the hospital. Even his mother approved of the idea.

Director Whittle was pleased, of course. He wanted to go on vacation and the presence of the biggest contributor would boost the finances of the hospital. Money would come pouring in. Jared Lowell's presence and influence would ensure that it did.

Jared wasn't a guy who flaunted his emotions publicly. To the world, he was this cool, slick, unfeeling, rich sonofabitch. Women found that irresistible. He discovered early that women were easily blinded by his wealth and good looks. There was no shortage of skirts who gladly threw themselves into his arms. He didn't care if they loved him or not. He never invested his heart in any one before. His money made up far more than what he was not willing to give.

But Chante was different. This was the first time any woman had ever turned him down. That confused him because he knew she was sexually attracted to him. That was pretty obvious after what happened between them the first night they met.

What did he say or do wrong that day on the roof deck to make her run away from him? That hurt him more than he cared to admit. He thought he was doing the right thing. That was the way he maneuvered all his past relationships.

When he saw her again last night, he was assailed with conflicting emotions. He felt an immense desire to take her into his arms and kiss her then. But he was afraid she'd run away again. So he played it cool.

Meeting that man, that Dr. Leo Cadman, at the lobby was unexpected. The way he put his arm across her shoulder like he owned her... he wanted to hit him right then and there. The way he looked at Chante like she was the most precious thing in the world. That annoyed him.

The thought that Chante went home and made love to him last night tormented him. He was intelligent enough to recognize that he was jealous. But he denied it vehemently. Jealousy was not supposed to be in his nature. How could it be? He never gave his heart away before.

He checked out Leo Cadman's record and found it outstanding. There was nothing he could fault him with. He found that very exasperating.

And now, he recognized all these thoughts in Chante's face. She was thinking of Leo Cadman and that made him feel cold all over.

Didn't she just kiss him back like he, Jared Lowell, was all that mattered to her?

Jared struggled with all these confusing emotions. One thing was certain. He wanted her to be around him long enough to unravel all the confusion that assaulted him.

"I'm sorry Chante. That was uncalled for. I think I missed you. Please don't run away again. I promise nothing will happen that you do not approve of." Jared said by way of explanation.

That was unexpected, Chante thought. Jared Lowell offering a truce was not something she saw coming.

"Ok…" Chante replied, hesitant yet appreciative for his concern.

That was a good start. She couldn't imagine what the next few days would be like if she had to resist him every time he made his advances. She knew she wanted that too, but there was Leo…

They spent the next few hours in easy camaraderie. Jared could be a joy to work with if he wasn't being the domineering person he was so used to being.

Chante found the hours flew by very fast and soon it was time to go.

"I assume the boyfriend is waiting for you at the lobby?"Jared teased her as she was preparing to leave.

"Yes…" Chante replied, suddenly realizing she was not looking forward to seeing Leo tonight at all.

"Well…ok then… let's not keep him waiting…" Jared replied.

Chante couldn't figure out the emotion she heard in his voice. Was he teasing her again? Why did he sound like he wasn't glad about that? She wanted to tell him that she'd rather stay here with him now, but the uneasy truce between them was so new. She didn't want anything to spoil it.

Chante hoped he would at least walk her down again to the lobby. She'd be happy just to have a precious few minutes more of his company.

But Jared turned away and made a move to pick up more documents on the table.

Chante felt a lump of disappointment in her throat. 'How easily he could dismiss her presence,' she thought.

She rode down the elevator feeling morose.

Leo was there waiting for her just as she thought. He was happy to see her again after missing out on their coffee break date.

He gave her a warm hug followed by a short passionate kiss. A few other nurses loitering about the lobby looked their way. Chante thought she saw envy in their eyes.

She should be feeling on top of the world, she mused. But she was assailed by guilt that was hard to explain. She tried her best to make her greeting at least sound as enthusiastic as he was.

"I've got a surprise for you," Leo whispered in her ear.

He ushered her out into his car that was parked by the sidewalk, opened the car door, and let her in.

Chante glance upward into the hospital building and thought she saw the silhouette of Jared outlined against one of the glass window of the 7th floor. Chante was sure he could see them from that window above.

Leo entered the car and revved up the engine. Soon they were cruising down the streets of New York City.

"Where're we going?" Chante inquired.

This wasn't the route home.

"You'll see when we get there," Leo answered mysteriously.

There was a noticeable gleam in his eyes as he reached for her hand before bringing it to his lips to kiss it. They drove in comfortable silence until they reached the café where they first had dinner.

"What could possibly be surprising about having dinner here?" Chante thought.

They have been here a couple of times more since that day.

The maître'd ushered them towards the rear of the café and out again through the back exit and into the darkness beyond.

"Leo…" Chante resisted at the hand that was pulling her forward.

She couldn't see anything up ahead except for the encompassing darkness.

Suddenly the darkness was illuminated by hundreds upon hundreds of glowing white bulbs. The trees were festooned with string lights bathing the place with an ethereal glow. It looked magical. And just beneath one of the trees was a table setting for two. A bottle of champagne nestled inside an ice bucket on top of the table.

"Oh Leo, this is so beautiful…" Chante cried out in wonder.

This was so typical of Leo… always trying to make her feel extra special.

"What are we celebrating tonight? Have you been promoted to ER Chief? What?" A clueless Chante asked.

Leo made a move to get something from his back pocket as Chante looked up at the trees around them.

When she glanced back at him, Leo was down on one knee. He held a small square box in his hand. He snapped the lid open, and without moving his eyes from her, took a small ring from inside the box and held it up for her to see.

Chante thought she was dreaming as she saw Leo holding up the ring and heard him say the words.

"I love you, Chante and I want to spend the rest of my life with you. Will you give me the honor of being my wife?" Leo said.

Chante was stunned beyond belief. This wasn't what she expected tonight… Leo down on his knees asking her to marry him. This was her dream after they seriously started dating one another. He was her dream come true. Dr. Leo Cadman was every girl's dream come true.

And here he was before her now, down on one knee, his face filled with promise to love her forever, and holding an engagement ring in his hand.

But why was she having difficulty seeing all that? Why was she seeing the face of Jared Lowell instead?

-To be continued in Book 3-

If you enjoyed this title, I would appreciate your leaving a review of the book. Good reviews encourage an author to write as well as help books to sell. Good reviews can be just a few short sentences describing what you liked about the book without having a spoiler. If you could spend 30 seconds writing a review, I would appreciate it: you can review this title right now at your favorite retailer.

Here is a preview of the **next book** you may also enjoy:

Love Abided: Audacious Billionaire BWWM Romance Series, Book 3

IT HAS been three weeks since the marriage proposal and Chante knew what she had to do. She knew it since the night she said 'yes' to Dr. Leo Cadman. Her sense of right and wrong had been bothering her like crazy since. It wasn't like she didn't have feelings for Leo. In her heart there was a special place for him. Even her common sense was telling her she did the right thing in accepting the ring. But how could she deny the little nagging voice telling her she was a fraud?

If it were just her and Leo in the equation, the conclusion would be a given. There was no doubt that he was the perfect man for her. She could learn to love him totally. But the existence of one Jared Lowell made the equation more complex than it should have been.

Considering that Jared hasn't even hinted about his true feelings- or any feeling for that matter- about her, Chante thought she was awfully stupid to feel guilty about accepting Leo's marriage proposal.

Couldn't she just consider Jared an infatuation and move on with her 'happily ever after' with an eligible doctor who obviously was crazy in love with her?

She knew the answer. If she was really honest with herself, she knew it all along. It wasn't like a bolt of lightning that just came out of the blue. She was in love with Jared and she had to tell Leo the truth. Whatever the consequences or outcome about her decision, she had to do it soon.

The engagement ring he had given her lay heavily in her left hand ring finger. She shouldn't even have worn it out onto the streets. The single solitaire diamond reflected the light from the street lamps she passed by.

She spotted a small café, entered the premises and sat at a barstool. The bar of the café faced a glass mirror looking out into the street. It was a small dive compared to the more glitzy ones but it was in Queens and near the home she shared with her brother, Markey. His sleeping meds had taken effect almost immediately and Chante took the time to go out into the fresh air and think about her dilemma.

Droplets of rain cascaded down the glass window as Chante let out a sigh of frustration.

"Swell…" she muttered under her breath.

Even the weather was a reflection of the guilt in her heart. It was a good thing Leo was gone for the entire week. He had to attend a medical conference in Atlanta, giving Chante precious time to work out how she would handle the situation when he came back. Initially he was hesitant to leave so soon after the proposal. He wanted to spend as much time as he could with her but Chante reassured him it was fine. The medical conference was a step forward in his career as an ER doctor.

But even Chante understood why she wanted him away. It would give her time to put her thoughts into perspective and she could only do that if she wasn't feeling so guilty about him being around her all the time.

She had to break the engagement. It wasn't fair to the guy. How could she pretend to love him when she knew that her feelings didn't go deep enough to deserve the ring he had given her?

And Jared was gone too. He left word that he would be gone for a few days to attend to some personal concerns. That left Chante feeling gloomy and abandoned, but also relieved that he didn't have to know about her current status – engaged to Dr. Leo Cadman.

She was hoping that by the time Jared got back, if he ever came back at all, she would have untangled herself from this farce of an engagement.

Right now, she felt trapped between a rock and a hard place, but one thing was for sure, she had to break an engagement that she was sure she couldn't live up to.

She probably would end up alone and miserable just the same, but at least her conscience wouldn't be nagging her day and night.

Chante ordered a beer and nursed her drink. She glanced at her watch and decided to drink up and head for home. The rain was now just a drizzle and she could sprint the few blocks home.

She pulled out her purse to pay the bill when a familiar voice greeted her.

"Well-well-well, if it isn't my favorite girl. Fancy meeting you here." The voice sneered.

Chante whirled swiftly around, a sudden fear creeping into her heart. She knew that voice.

"Oh… hi Jimmy…," Chante addressed him with a squeaky voice.

The new arrival was Jimmy Derollo, her ex-boyfriend. The guy always gave her the creeps. Chante wondered what she ever saw in him. Even now as he sidled towards her in the bar, she felt her skin crawl and the hair on the back of her neck stand on end.

Their last confrontation weeks ago on the sidewalk while waiting for the bus was something Chante wanted to forget. The hard slap she gave him on the face after he tried to kiss her still resounded in her ear. She vaguely remembered the threat he made as she swiftly boarded the bus. But she couldn't forget the murderous look in his eyes as the bus pulled away from him.

The bar was half-full and Chante knew that Jimmy wouldn't try anything stupid. One scream and even the bartender would probably come to her rescue. Still…she wasn't sure if she could deal with him once she was outside the confines of the bar. He could follow her home and she came alone.

If you enjoyed this sample then look for **Love Abided: Audacious Billionaire BWWM Romance Series, Book 3.**

Here is a preview of **another story** you may enjoy:

Love Evaded - Ardent Billionaire Romance Series, Book 2

"**DEIRDRE, I** love that new top." Cassie grinned as Deirdre walked out of the bathroom. It was a Friday night and Deirdre had a date with her new boyfriend, Felix.

"Thanks Cass," Deirdre answered, smoothing the silk fabric of her new peach tunic. The color looked amazing against Deirdre's skin; her plain, black slacks and ballet flats completed the outfit nicely.

"Where is Felix taking you?"

"We're going to try that new Thai place, near the college," Deirdre explained. "Felix has a late class tonight, so I'm meeting him there.

Deirdre had met Felix at the art college where she posed for classes. She'd started by modeling for hobby photographers, but over the last several weeks she'd sat for painters, sketch artists, and sculptors. She'd been offered the job after she'd gone to Simon, the photography instructor, and told him about the teenager at the hibachi restaurant who'd somehow ended up with one of her nude photos.

Simon had been outraged, and had assigned his graduate student Felix to get to the bottom of the situation. Felix had researched everyone in the hobby class, and found that only one had a teenaged son. Simon himself had visited the middle-aged student, and alerted him to the fact that his son was going through his things. The instructor left with all of Deirdre's photos; Felix had gathered photos from the rest of the students, to ensure that Deirdre would never be put in that position again. Simon changed his class policies; only works that didn't depict the model's face could be kept by their creators. Most of the students were sympathetic to the reasons behind the new policy, and many began sketching and painting the faces of their classmates onto Deirdre's body.

After the new policy went into effect, Deirdre happily agreed to pose whenever Simon needed her. On her second trip to the school, Felix asked her out on a date. The graduate student was kind, genuine and thoughtful, and Deirdre hated herself for thinking of Parker Hamlin when she was with him.

A month had passed since the last time she'd seen the gorgeous billionaire, but his face still haunted her thoughts. That morning at his studio, she'd been convinced that he was falling in love with her. She'd already allowed herself to fall in love with him. But then, just as she'd feared, he'd decided that she wasn't the type of person he wanted to be with. Ironically, the job that had brought her to Felix was the same job that had made Parker walk away. Deirdre still wondered what her life would be like now if they hadn't run into that teenager. She sighed out loud.

"What's the matter, Dee?" Cassie asked knowingly.

"Nothing," she replied quickly. Deirdre knew exactly what her best friend would say if she knew that Parker was still in her thoughts.

"Are you sure? You seem distracted… pensive even."

"I'm just stressed about school, Cass," Deirdre assured her. "I feel like I'm never going to finish."

"It'll take as long as it takes, Dee. It doesn't matter when you graduate. It just matters that you keep working at it."

"That's nice of you to say, but it does matter. The sooner I finish school, the sooner I can get a better job and move D'Angelo to a better neighborhood." Thoughts of her brother's safety were always at the forefront of Deirdre's mind.

"You'll feel better next semester," Cassie assured her, "when you're on campus."

Deirdre smiled at the thought of going to real, live lectures as opposed to online classes. She'd managed to land another weekly singing gig that paid better than her Thursdays at Fuseli's. That, combined with her regular modeling sessions at the art college, had made it possible for her to quit her job at the hotel. She'd be able to spend most of the summer home with D'Angelo, and start classes on campus in August.

"Would you have ever thought that my saving grace would come from Carl?" Deirdre laughed. Her ex-boyfriend Carl had been the one who had found her the modeling job.

"Yeah, I bet if he'd known you'd hook-up with Felix, he'd have never set you up in the job." Cassie laughed. "But that's Carl for you. He never thinks things through. I still can't believe what happened to him."

Deirdre nodded. Towards the end of her relationship with Carl, she'd suspected that he was involved with one of the local gangs. After she left him, he'd stopped trying to hide what he was up to. He'd even tried to use her apartment as a stash pad for his illegal activities. Deirdre had refused, and two weeks ago Carl had been arrested for possession of stolen goods and a laundry list of illegal substances. The other gang members were perfectly happy to let Carl take the fall, and word on the street was that he was looking at forty years in a federal penitentiary.

"Maybe he and my mother can reconnect," Deirdre said flatly.

"Have you talked to her recently?" Cassie pressed. Deirdre hardly ever talked about her mother, and talked to her even less.

"I send her pictures of D'Angelo. He used to write letters to send along with them, but he doesn't anymore. She writes once a week… apologizes, says she's changed. She's even found God, apparently. But I don't have anything to say to her."

"Well, we have more important things to think about, don't we?" Cassie smiled. She'd been friends with Deirdre since grade school, and was almost as hurt by Pauline's drug use as her children were. "You need to get going, you don't want to make Felix wait."

Deirdre took one last look in the mirror, kissed D'Angelo goodbye, and rushed out the door.

<<◇>>

Deirdre arrived at the small, storefront restaurant and saw Felix's Audi already in the parking lot. She walked through the door and found him sitting at a small, private booth near the back wall. She smiled broadly as she walked over to join him, and he rose to greet her.

"You look beautiful." He smiled as he leaned down and kissed her cheek.

"Thanks," she offered graciously, "how was your class?"

Felix sighed. "It's a freshman level humanities class… no one is there because they want to be, they're there because they have to be. And that includes yours truly." He shrugged.

Deirdre sat across the table, studying her date. Felix was tall and lanky, with blue eyes and curly auburn hair that hung down over his ears. He was attractive in that free-spirited, down-to-earth way. Felix was in his final year of the art college's Masters of Arts program. An artistic genius, he'd attended a progressive liberal arts high school that allowed him to take college art courses. He'd received his bachelor's degree just one year after officially graduating high school; he was on track to finish his master's degree at only twenty-two.

"I'll be teaching what I want to teach soon enough." Felix smiled. "How has your day been? How was D'Angelo's awards assembly?"

Deirdre smiled, surprised that he'd remembered. The last day of school awards assembly at D'Angelo's school had been that morning. Deirdre had mentioned it to Felix only once, and that had been at least two weeks ago.

"It was fantastic." She beamed. "D'Angelo got the Presidential Award for Academic Excellence, and also the Presidential Fitness award. He was the only one in his class who got both. He's ready to make you pay up on his report card too, he has straight A's."

Felix whistled. "And I said ten bucks an A, right? I may have to renegotiate my price for next year or that kid is going to break me," he teased.

Deirdre felt incredibly lucky to have found Felix, if for no other reason than the fact that he was so good with D'Angelo. Felix had lost his own parents in a car accident when he was ten, and afterward his older brother and sister-in-law had raised him. He understood the boy's situation better than Deirdre could ever hope to.

If you enjoyed this sample then look for **Love Evaded - Ardent Billionaire Romance Series, Book 2.**

Here is a preview of **another story** you may enjoy:

Love Bound - Lonely Billionaire Romance Series, Book 2

TRICIA SAT in her childhood home and gazed at the wall; today had been particularly trying. In addition to flying from Seattle to Dallas, she had immediately started to take care of her mother. Diagnosed with Alzheimer's, her mother also had a heart condition, and like always, had refused to take any medicine.

Before she had moved to Texas, her mother had lived in Alabama where she saw the effects of the Tuskegee Experiment that lasted long after the experiment had officially ended. African-American men who were diagnosed with syphilis in the 1930s were tracked for forty years to see the long-term effects of the disease. Even when a cure came out in the 1950s, the doctors had not cured the men. Instead, they told patients who wanted to be treated that they had already been given medicine. Hundreds and thousands of people from the families were infected and affected by the trial.

Due to this, Tricia's mother refused to listen to white doctors. The crotchety old woman refused to believe that medicine would help or that anything was wrong with her. After an hour of trying and failing to convince her mother to take the medicine, Tricia had finally given up. She had made some bread pudding with dinner and sprinkled crumbled tablets into her mother's portions. It may not have been the most honest solution, but it worked. Now, Tricia was just exhausted.

Moving back to the kitchen, she started to make herself a cup of chamomile tea. With her mother in bed, it was time to drink some tea and unwind. Thankfully, she only had another two days until the weekend. Her brother Tyrone had promised to take care of her mother over the weekend so that Tricia could take a break and catch up with some old friends.

Sipping her cup of tea, she went to the bathroom and turned on the bathwater. As bubbles and warm water filled the tub, she slowly began to remove her clothes. Only a few days ago, she had left John. After telling him of her decision to return home to her mother, she had not talked to him or seen him again. Their brief fling had been as passionate as it was short-lived. She had taken care of his wife during the final stages of ALS.

Although they had tried to stop their sexual desires from taking over, John and Tricia had made love more than a couple of times. It was wrong and she still felt guilty. Despite her ethical concerns, she found herself wishing that she was still with him. His confident nature and unwavering conscience had attracted her to him from the moment they met.

Easing herself into the water, Tricia laughed to herself. If only her mother knew that she had slept with a rich, white man. She would never forgive her. Tricia picked up Jane Eyre and tried to read, but even her favorite novel could not distract her mind. She wanted John more than anything. It was impossible for her to go without sex anymore. After realizing how fulfilling and satisfying sex could be with him, she was not willing to go back to her normal celibate lifestyle.

She glanced at the bathroom door and saw that it was locked. Moving her hand down her body, she closed her eyes and pretended that her hand was John's. Tricia ran her fingertips around the dark cocoa-colored skin around her nipples and then drew it down further. Initially, she started playing with the soft lips around her clit. This was not enough to satisfy her for long. She moved her clit in slow circles as she imagined John entering her for the first time in the office. The sex had been so magnetic, so electrically charged. She imagined his hard muscles moving against her and moaned.

The moan startled her. She looked at the door to see if her mother had heard anything. There were no sounds from the rest of the house. Moving her hand down along her body again, she moved her fingers faster and faster. Tricia could feel herself approaching orgasm when a sudden sound surprised her. The shrill ringing of the phone pierced the air.

For a moment, Tricia thought about ignoring it and finishing herself off. With a belabored sigh, she stood up and grabbed a towel. It could be someone important for her mother.

Exiting the bathroom, she rushed to reach the phone before it stopped ringing. "Hello?" she said with a breathy voice…

If you enjoyed this sample then look for **Love Bound - Lonely Billionaire Romance Series, Book 2**.

Other Books by Shyla Starr

- Persuasive Billionaire BWWM Romance Series

- Tenacious Billionaire BWWM Romance Series

- Elusive Billionaire Romance Series

- Lonely Billionaire Romance Series

- Ardent Billionaire Romance Series

- Fervent Billionaire BWWM Romance Series

Get the latest update on new releases from the author at:

https://shylastarr.com/newsletter/

About the Author - Shyla Starr

Shyla currently specializes in writing interracial romance stories and is a huge fan of the alpha male. Simply put, there just aren't enough stories about mixed couple romances, which is something she is aiming to fix.

Being a bookworm all her life, when Shyla discovered men she also realized how easy it was to fulfill her fantasies through her writing.

When not writing and fantasizing about men, Shyla enjoys dancing, reading and chilling with her friends.

Connect with Shyla Starr

I really appreciate you reading my book! Here are my social media coordinates:

Friend me on Facebook:
https://www.facebook.com/shylastarrauthor

Follow me on Twitter: https://twitter.com/shylstarr

Check me out on Goodreads:
https://www.goodreads.com/author/show/8436084.Shyla_Starr

Subscribe to my newsletter:
https://shylastarr.com/newsletter/

Visit my website: https://shylastarr.com/

www.ingramcontent.com/pod-product-compliance
Lightning Source LLC
Chambersburg PA
CBHW030822200726
48288CB00004B/1356